BOOKS BY PHYLLIS REYNOLDS NAYLOR

Witch's Sister
Witch Water
The Witch Herself
Walking Through the Dark
How I Came to Be a Writer
How Lazy Can You Get?
Eddie, Incorporated

EDDIE,
INCORPORATED

Phyllis Reynolds Naylor

EDDIE,
INCORPORATED

AN ALADDIN BOOK
Atheneum

Published by Atheneum
All rights reserved
Text copyright © 1980 by Phyllis Reynolds Naylor
Illustrations copyright © 1980 by Blanche Sims
Published simultaneously in Canada by McClelland & Stewart Ltd.
Manufactured by Fairfield Graphics
Fairfield, Pennsylvania
ISBN: 0-689-71036-4
First Aladdin Edition

To Mike,
dreamer, schemer, and inventor,
with love

Contents

EDDIE,
INCORPORATED

ONE

Family Business

EDDIE WATCHED his father over the meatballs. Mr. Anselmino and Roger were discussing net profits. Roger worked in a shoe store, and every evening when he came home to dinner, he talked about percentages.

Across the table, Eddie's other brother, Joseph, was holding a pocket calculator in his lap. He was eating green beans with one hand and pushing buttons with the other.

Eddie knew what Joseph was doing: he was figuring the interest on the fifty dollars and forty-three cents he had in the bank. Every day he figured the interest, and every day it came out a fraction more. Then he would figure how much his money would earn if he left it there for five years, or eleven years, or sixty years.

"Not at the table!" said Mrs. Anselmino, taking in everybody at once with a huge sweep of her gray eyes. "This is a family, not a corporation."

Joseph put the calculator under his chair, Roger picked up his fork, and Mr. Anselmino turned to Eddie.

"So how was school?" he said.

EDDIE WANTED A JOB. Not a sort-the-laundry or clean-the-garage or scrub-the-sinks job; he wanted a business. He wanted a desk with a phone on it; a rubber stamp with his name on it; a book for expenses, and a box for cash receipts. He wanted to be a boss.

The Anselminos were a business family, no matter how much Mrs. Anselmino tried to keep shop talk away from the table. Eddie's father owned a produce store. In the fall and winter, you could open the big green door there on Lexington Avenue and be drowned in the fragrance of crisp, juicy apples. There were boxes of them, crates of them, a crazy quilt of yellow and red, and if you wanted to know the difference between a winesap and a McIntosh, Eddie's father could describe it exactly.

In the spring, the apples gave way to strawberries, and early peas, and long pink stalks of rhubarb. But in the summer, the awnings were up and the fruit was displayed outdoors. Bees tasted first the grapes and then the peaches and plums that were as big as Eddie's fist.

Trucks would roll up to the back of the store with their cargo of watermelons and potatoes and cantaloupe and squash, and Mr. Anselmino would watch them unload, checking off things on a clipboard. There were five other people working for him in his store, and on Fridays Mr. Anselmino would pay them their wages. On Christmas, he gave them each a box of pears.

Mrs. Anselmino, too, had a business. Every Tuesday she brought into the store the things that she had made at home—the jellies, the jams, the rhubarb pies, the banana bread—and whenever a clerk sold something that Eddie's mother had made, it was recorded in a book. On Fridays, Mrs. Anselmino got a share of the profits.

Roger Anselmino, who was twenty-two, worked for the Rite-Fit Shoe Store. He had begun as a stock boy, worked his way up to salesman, and had finally been promoted to assistant manager. He had already decided that before he was thirty, he would become manager himself and buy stock in the company.

Rite-Fit Shoe Store was in the heart of downtown, and thousands of people passed it every day. In the show window, on a pedestal, was a plaster cast of a foot wearing a see-through shoe to prove that Rite-Fit shoes never pinched the toes or rubbed

the heels. Roger was in charge of the show window, and every Monday he put up a new display.

Joseph, who was three years older than Eddie, was going to be a banker. He had known what he wanted to be ever since his fourth birthday when somebody gave him a toy cash register. He never had to sit around and worry about what he'd be when he was grown. He was already taking typing in school so that he could type out checks. Next year he would take a course called "Basic Bookkeeping," and the year after that, an introductory course in shorthand. He had even opened an account at the First National Bank of Detroit to make a good impression when he applied for a job there in ten years.

While Eddie read the sports pages of the paper, Joseph read the real estate ads; when Eddie looked over the TV guide, Joseph browsed through the business articles; and by the time Eddie had reached the comics, Joseph was checking the Dow Jones average in the financial section.

Everybody, it seemed, was going places and doing things except Eddie.

EDDIE WORRIED about a lot of things. He wasn't strong and sturdy like his father. Mr. Anselmino's hands were as big as cabbages, and he could lift two bushels of potatoes at one time. Eddie still wore

Buster Brown mittens, and the most he had ever lifted off the truck was a watermelon.

Eddie wasn't artistic like his mother. Mrs. Anselmino didn't just make a pie or cake; she created a masterpiece. The edges were fluted like ceramic tile, the pecans were all pointing the same direction, and chocolate glaze dribbled over vanilla icing in a gorgeous array of concentric circles. When she labeled her jams and jellies, she used a camel-hair brush and India ink, and the letters looked as though they had been taken from a prayer book in a Spanish church. When Eddie tried to draw something, he always had to explain it to people. They never said, "Great!" or "Fantastic!" or even "Beautiful!" Instead, they frowned, coughed, and ended up by saying "Tell me about it, Eddie."

Eddie wasn't energetic like Roger, either. Roger got up at six every morning even though he didn't have to be at the shoe store till nine. He put on his warm-up suit and jogged three times around the high school and then came home and worked out some more in the basement. When Eddie woke up in the morning, it was all he could do to keep his left eye open while he crawled around under the bed looking for yesterday's tee-shirt.

As for Joseph, Eddie wasn't like him at all. He didn't even look like him. Joseph's hair came neatly down over his ears and curled gently down the nape of his neck. Eddie's hair grew in short black tufts that stuck out at various angles from his head. Joseph liked puzzles and problems and quizzes. He liked spelling bees and math marathons and essay contests. He was always making charts of how high he could jump or how far he could run or how many words he could type before making a mistake. His room was filled with bits of paper with scores and averages, and almost nothing made him happier than doing something two points better than he'd done it the day before.

Almost nothing would make Eddie happier than a job.

"Don't worry about it, kid," Roger always told him. "There's a place for you somewhere."

But Eddie worried anyway. If he didn't find his place soon, somebody else might take it. If he didn't decide what kind of work he wanted to do now, how would he know what to study when he got to high school? He might end up raising sheep or something. How could he even go looking for a job if he didn't have a car? But how could he buy a car if he didn't have any money? And how could he get any money if he didn't have a job?

It all seemed so hopeless that Eddie hardly knew what to worry about first. He worried about inflation and recession and income tax evasion because he heard Roger talk about them at the table, but he didn't know what they meant. And because he didn't know what they meant, they scared him all the more.

"Oh, Eddie, Eddie, just be yourself," his mother would say when he tried to talk to her about it, and she would hug him with her huge arms. And Eddie, struggling to breathe, would have loved to just "be himself" if he only knew what it was he could do best. But how could he find out what he could do unless he had a job to prove it?

He finally decided that if he was ever going to amount to anything, he would have to go into business for himself. In fact, that was the very best kind of business to have. He would be his own boss, there would be no one around to tell him what to do, and he certainly wouldn't have to worry about getting fired.

TWO

Dink and Others

THE ONE CONSOLATION was that Dink and Elizabeth didn't have jobs yet either. They were Eddie's two best friends in a neighborhood of at least one hundred and eighty-nine children.

Most of the children were younger than Eddie. When they came in to Mr. Anselmino's produce store, their heads were barely visible above the melons. It was hard to know they were there until a hand reached up for a grape. If Eddie didn't watch where he was going, he was likely to step on them, and if he didn't step on them, he was likely to sit on them. Mr. Anselmino could never lock up at night until he was sure that no one was hiding in the potato bin.

Every week it seemed that another baby had been added to a household somewhere. And what began as a sweet little baby who lay on its back and cooed turned into a big, strong baby later on, with fists like steel clamps. The O'Conner baby, in fact, also known as Herman the Terrible, was so bold and so powerful that whenever he was wheeled into the produce store, the clerks covered up all the cherries before he could get at them.

Dink and Elizabeth were Eddie's refuge from the baby boom. And they worried too, but about different things. Elizabeth wanted to be an airline pilot when she grew up, and wondered if she could follow a map. Eddie tried to tell her that she would have charts and radar and everything, but she still worried now and then that if it were foggy, she might not be able to tell New Jersey from Delaware.

When Dink worried, he worried about teeth —false teeth—and whether or not he'd get them. His grandfather had them and his father had them, and his mother had an upper plate that she took out and put on her dresser at night. The only thing Dink worried about more than wearing false teeth was getting drafted. If he could stay out of the army and keep away from false teeth, Dink thought he could be happy.

To Eddie and his friends, it seemed that the world was divided between adults who already knew how to do income tax, follow a map, and floss their teeth, and little grubby people who were too young to worry at all. Eddie and Dink and Elizabeth were caught in the middle—old enough to know about all sorts of problems ahead, but too young to do anything about them. It was a wonder, Eddie decided, that people didn't have heart attacks in sixth grade.

THERE WAS SOMETHING SPECIAL about Mr. Clemmons next door—something besides the way his ears stuck out on either side of his large, bald head. He was an inventor of sorts and had a workshop next to Mr. Anselmino's garage.

Eddie went over to Mr. Clemmons' to talk about going into business for himself.

The inventor was standing at his workbench holding a piece of garden hose in one hand. One end of the hose was attached to a gallon jar of yucky-looking water, and the other was fastened to a little metal cage.

"Hello, Eddie," said Mr. Clemmons, without even looking at him. He turned the gallon bottle upside down. The icky-looking water came gushing through the garden hose, into the cage at the other end, and shot out through the holes in the mesh, collecting in a basin underneath.

Mr. Clemmons gave it his full attention. When all the water was out, he carefully examined the cage. It was full of string and hair and lint, and there was only a small amount of fuzz in the basin.

He smiled happily. "Well, Eddie, what do you think of that?"

Eddie hardly knew what to think because he didn't even know what it was.

"Tell me about it," he said finally, sorry he couldn't think of anything better.

Mr. Clemmons pointed to the gallon jar. "This," he said, "is your mother's washing machine."

"It is?" said Eddie.

"And this," said Mr. Clemmons, "is the hose that connects it to the sink."

He picked up a bucket that had even more yucky-looking water in it, filled the bottle again, and put the hose back on it.

"Now," he said, "the water from your mother's washing machine goes through a hose and into the basement sink. If all the lint from the laundry goes down the drain, the pipe will eventually clog up and you'll have to call a plumber."

He folded his arms across his chest, still beaming. "Do you know what your mother does to keep that from happening?"

"No," said Eddie, wondering how Mr. Clemmons knew either.

"Your mother . . . *everybody's* mother . . . all the women in Detroit," Mr. Clemmons said, spreading his arms wide, "tie one of their old stockings to the end of the hose to catch the lint, and when the stocking gets full, they throw it away and put on another."

Eddie was surprised that Mr. Clemmons knew so much about the women of Detroit when he hardly ever went out of his shop.

"Do you know what's the matter with stockings?" the inventor went on. "I'll tell you what's the matter with stockings. First, old stockings have holes in them, because if they didn't have holes they wouldn't have been thrown out. Right? Right. So some of the lint gets through the holes and down the drain anyway. Second, it takes a lot of stockings to keep lint out of the sink. Some women don't even have that many old stockings. And sometimes . . ." He rolled his eyes. *"Sometimes* the stocking gets so full that it bursts. *Pow!* Water and string and lint and fuzz all over the place!"

He picked up the wire cage at the other end of the garden hose. "This is going to protect your mother from all that. This is going to be known as the Clemmons Lint Catcher, and I'm going to sell it to every hardware store in the country. The only problem is that some lint gets through, so I've got to work on it a little more, make the mesh a little finer, and then . . . *then* . . . !"

"I'm going into business, too," said Eddie.

"No kidding?" Mr. Clemmons sat down on his stool and reached for the cup of cold coffee that he kept at the back of his workbench. "What kind of business?"

"Well, I haven't really decided yet. I'm sort of looking around."

"First," said Mr. Clemmons, "there has to be a problem. Find a problem, and you've got yourself a business. It's as simple as that."

EDDIE THOUGHT about it when he left the workshop and went around the alley toward home. He saw an empty soda can in front of him and gave it a kick, sending it flying down the concrete. Three steps further on, there was another one, and then another. The place looked like a dump. It was getting to be a real problem, Mrs. Anselmino had said just that morning.

A problem! Eddie stopped. That was it! He'd start an aluminum recycling business. He'd get Dink and Elizabeth to help. They'd go around collecting aluminum cans, wash them, flatten them, bag them, and turn them in for money. They'd tell all their friends about it—Billy Watson, Janice Pringle, and all the kids at school. Everyone would be saving cans.

His head whirled in dizzy happiness. Eagerly

he grabbed up all the aluminum cans he could, wedged open the back screen with his foot, and took them down to the basement where the Anselmino Aluminum Recycling Company was about to begin.

His mother's washing machine stood in one corner. A hose from somewhere in back of the washer hung over the edge of the sink. And there on the end of the hose, fastened tightly with a rubber band, was one of Mrs. Anselmino's stockings.

Mr. Clemmons was a genius.

THREE

Profits and Partners

THE SOUTH END MIDDLE SCHOOL was composed of sixth, seventh, and eighth graders instead of the usual junior high arrangement. Every noon, the students had an hour off for something called activity period. During this time they ate their lunch and afterwards they could walk around, talk with teachers, use the library, and go outside and throw frisbees.

Eddie called a business conference during activity period. While their other sixth-grade friends were shooting baskets over on the concrete, Eddie, Dink, and Elizabeth sat on the wall at the driveway entrance and had a meeting.

It was understood from the beginning that they were partners. They would all three be bosses, so nobody could tell them what to do.

"We've got to have advertising," said Eddie.

Elizabeth lifted her face toward the warm May

sun and closed her eyes for a moment. She wore huge, round, blue-tinted glasses, and her hair was pulled up in a large topknot.

"What we need," she said, "is to rent a plane that would fly all over Detroit trailing a banner that said, 'Anselmino's Aluminum Recycling Now Open for Business.' "

She even looked like an executive.

"Elizabeth can do advertising," said Eddie, and knew she'd think of something, even without the plane. "We also need someone in charge of supply— to find out where the cans are and go after them."

"I could use Dad's garbage can carrier and go around collecting," Dink said. He was wearing a tee-shirt with Godzilla on the front. He didn't look like an executive, but he did look as though he could walk over half of Detroit pushing a one-hundred pound load.

"You've got it," said Eddie. "Vice-president in charge of supply."

"Hey, Eddie," Billy Watson called. "Let's shoot a few baskets."

"Not now," said Eddie. "We've got business."

EDDIE HIMSELF was in charge of the factory, which was half the Anselmino's basement. He set up a card table with a clock and a pen and a notebook on it.

He propped up a long piece of rain gutter under the basement window as a chute, a packing box to catch the cans, a tub to rinse them in, a hair dryer to dry them, a sledge hammer to flatten them, and a box of leaf bags to bind them up in five-pound bundles.

All week long Elizabeth went about the neighborhood tacking handmade posters on telephone poles. The announcement read:

Tired of litter?
Sick of junk?
ANSELMINO'S ALUMINUM RECYCLING COMPANY
needs your old cans

And then it listed Eddie's address and phone number.

Dink had painted a big OPEN sign on the back of a dart board to set up outside the house. The Anselmino Aluminum Recycling Company would begin its first day of business on Saturday, May 17, at nine o'clock.

"I'll be here at eight-thirty, in case there's a line," Elizabeth said to Eddie on Friday.

"And we ought to put in a night deposit box so people will have some place to put their cans after we're closed," Dink suggested. He said he would make one and bring it with him on Saturday.

Even Joseph was interested in the company.

"How much can you get for aluminum cans, Eddie?" he asked at dinner.

"Seventeen cents a pound."

Joseph figured it out on the calculator he had wedged between his leg and the seat of his chair. "Only five hundred and eighty-eight pounds and you'll have a hundred dollars," he said, and went on to figure the interest.

"What are you going to do with the profits?" Roger asked Eddie. "Have you thought of investing it somewhere? The bank gives five and one half percent."

Actually, Eddie had been thinking of putting it in the back of his top dresser drawer under the extra shoelaces, but he said he'd consider investing.

"And what about Dink and Elizabeth?" Mr. Anselmino asked. "Are you putting them on salary, or do they share the profits?"

Eddie wasn't sure.

"If they're on salary," his father said, "that means you pay them a certain amount each week regardless of how much the company takes in. If the company loses money, you'll have to pay them out of your allowance or something. But if the company makes money, they still get only their salary and you get all the rest."

It wasn't difficult to decide that one. Eddie,

Dink, and Elizabeth were a team. It would be share and share alike. Even if they made a hundred dollars the first day, they'd split it three ways.

"We're sharing the profits," he said, and realized he was beginning to sound like Roger. It was a good feeling, especially when he understood what he was talking about.

"Who's going to pay for the leaf bags you took out of the tool shed?" asked Mrs. Anselmino.

"We'll take it out of our earnings," Eddie told her. They hadn't even opened for business and already they were sixty-three cents in debt.

HE WOKE AT FIVE the next morning and looked out the window to see if a line was forming yet. The street was still dark and empty. He knew he wouldn't sleep anymore, so he got up, dressed, and went out on the porch to wait.

The paper boy came by, followed by his dog. The mutt was holding something in his mouth that looked familiar. Eddie went down the steps and took it away from him. It was one of the advertisements for the Anselmino Aluminum Recycling Company.

"Hey, where'd he get this?" Eddie called after the boy.

The paper boy shrugged. "I don't know. It was blowing around on the street back there."

Eddie went down to the corner. The poster had been ripped off the telephone pole. There was still a piece of it left. He walked over to the next street. That poster was there, but someone had drawn two tanks on it, having a war, with smoke and bombs all over the words. At the next telephone pole, someone had crossed out Eddie's telephone number and scribbled in the number for the fire department instead.

He went back home and sat on the steps. This neighborhood didn't have too many old cans; it had too many rotten children. Anselmino's Children Recycling Company, that's what it ought to be. They ought to go around collecting bratty kids in Dink's garbage cart, weigh them in, tie them in sacks, and send them off to Siberia.

Mrs. Anselmino found Eddie still on the porch at seven o'clock and made him come in for breakfast. She put a plate of scrambled eggs before him and a sausage and an English muffin and then, on the spur of the moment, she poured him a half cup of coffee and filled the cup up with cream.

"Now," she said, "you're ready for business."

He was beginning to feel good again.

Dink and Elizabeth arrived at eight-thirty. Dink had brought a night-deposit box made out of a Baskin Robbins ice cream container. On the curb at the end of the driveway he placed the dart board sign saying, OPEN.

At five minutes till nine, they took their places —Dink outside the basement window, Elizabeth at the bottom of the chute, and Eddie at the card table desk.

On the top of the first page of his notebook, Eddie wrote, "The Anselmino Aluminum Recycling Company" and, as an afterthought, added, "Incorporated," though he wasn't sure what it meant.

Underneath, he made six vertical columns with a ruler. At the top of the first column he wrote, "Date." At the top of the second, he wrote "Number of cans." At the top of the third, "Number of pounds." At the fourth, "Income," the fifth, "Expenses," and at the top of the final column he wrote "Profit." Then, after a moment, he added, ". . . or Loss."

FOUR

The Last of the Pabst Blue Ribbon

NINE O'CLOCK CAME, nine-fifteen, and at twenty after, Dink yelled, "Somebody's coming!"

There were footsteps on the driveway outside, and the sound of the mailman's voice. He wanted to know where the aluminum deposit was, and Dink directed him to the open window.

The sleeve of a blue uniform came through the window and deposited one empty iced tea can in the rain gutter.

Clunk-ity . . . clunk-ity . . . thunk.

It was a very lonely sound. The iced tea can lay all by itself in the bottom of the packing box, and the blue uniform disappeared.

Elizabeth picked up the can and dropped it in the water in the wash tub, placed it under the hair dryer for a minute, and then flattened it with the sledge hammer.

"One," she said, as she set it over against the wall.

Eddie made a mark in the second column of his notebook beside May 17.

About ten o'clock, Mr. Clemmons came over with an armload of cans he had picked up in the alley. He dropped them down the chute one after another: *clunkity, clunkity, thumpity, bang, thud.* It was a beautiful noise.

"Hey, thanks a lot!" said Dink outside the window.

Now it was more like a factory. Elizabeth had barely taken all the cans out of the packing box when Dink's mother came around to the window and deposited a few Dr. Pepper cans and seven Sprites. There were cans in the packing case at the bottom of the chute, cans floating about in the wash tub, cans under the hair dryer, and cans waiting to be smashed.

"This is more like it," said Eddie.

THINGS SLOWED A LITTLE over the lunch hour. Mrs. Anselmino brought down some salami sandwiches, and they took turns eating and standing out on the driveway to direct people to the deposit window.

Billy Watson and some boys from the South End Middle School rode over on their bikes, stuck their heads in the window and yelled crazy things. One of them rolled a rock down the chute. But after they went away, Elizabeth's father arrived with two grocery sacks full of cans.

"Way to go!" whooped Dink from outside as he poured the cans down the rain gutter.

Eddie and Elizabeth were working as fast as they could.

About three o'clock the hair dryer began to smell funny, and Eddie decided that maybe it needed a rest, so they finished drying the cans with a towel.

At four, old Mrs. Harris came by pulling a little wagon. It was piled high with cans, and she stooped down outside the window and began dropping them one at a time down the chute.

Eddie and Elizabeth stared. There were baked bean cans and creamed corn cans and scalloped potato cans and about twenty fruit cocktail. Only one of the cans was aluminum; the rest were tin, and the baked bean can still had a frankfurter in the bottom.

"Why didn't you stop her, Dink?" Elizabeth called up after the woman had left.

"I didn't have the heart," he said. "She pulled that wagon four blocks, so I just thanked her, and she said there were more cans where those came from."

At five o'clock, Eddie took the OPEN sign and put it behind the house. He closed the basement window and put the night deposit box in front of it. Then he and Dink and Elizabeth went back to the basement to tally up the day's profits.

There were one-hundred and thirty-six cans. Eddie brought down the bathroom scale to see how many pounds that would be. They began putting the flattened cans on the scale one at a time.

The marker barely moved. Three cans . . . four cans. . . .

"Maybe the scale is broken," said Elizabeth.

Around ten cans, they could tell that the marker had moved halfway between zero and one. It took twenty-one cans to make a pound.

Carefully they divided the cans into little heaps of twenty-one each. Six piles of cans with ten left over. Six pounds of cans at seventeen cents a pound.

Eddie went to his desk and figured it out. One dollar and two cents. He entered it under "income." Then he remembered the sixty-three cents they owed for the leaf bags and put that in the column marked "expenses." One dollar and two cents minus sixty-three cents left a profit of thirty-nine cents. And thirty-nine cents divided between Eddie, Dink, and Elizabeth was thirteen cents apiece.

"At least you didn't go in the hole," Mr. Ansel-, mino said at dinner that evening.

"And people know where to bring the cans now," said Roger.

"And he paid off his debt to me the very first day," said Mrs. Anselmino.

Joseph had not brought his pocket calculator to the table that evening, but Eddie could tell, by the way he pressed his fingers against the table top one at a time, that he was figuring something out in his head. "Thirteen cents a day, six days a week, fifty-two times a year, at five and a half percent . . ." he was saying to himself.

But Eddie wasn't interested in what he could make if the Anselmino Aluminum Recycling Company lasted a year. He was wondering if it would last a month. Eight hours a day for only thirteen cents was just a little more than one-and-a-half cents an hour, which meant he'd have to work a day and then some just to afford a stamp to mail his income tax. Bosses had more problems than anybody.

A FRIEND AT SCHOOL decided to stop collecting beer cans and told Eddie that he would give him his entire collection. As soon as the bell rang for activity period on Monday, Eddie, Dink, and Elizabeth ran out to the flagpole, and in a few minutes the boy came up the school driveway dragging a huge dry-cleaning bag loaded with beer cans.

"A whole year's collection," he said, and for a moment looked as though he didn't want to let go. "Well, it's yours now," he said finally, and walked off quickly before he could change his mind.

Eddie and his friends went through the side door and up the stairs to the second floor. The corridor was empty. Most of the students were in the cafeteria.

He opened his locker and tried to stuff the top of the bag inside, but the bottom ballooned out. Dink shoved at the bottom and the top puffed out. The plastic bag was partially filled with air, and it felt like a punching bag.

"Help push, Elizabeth," panted Eddie. "I think we've almost got it."

Elizabeth shoved with all her strength, trying to wedge the bulky bag in among Eddie's jacket and track shoes and tennis racket.

Pow! The bag exploded. Out tumbled Coors cans and Budweiser cans, Meister Bräu, Millers, and Schlitz. Pilsner and Fox Deluxe cans went cascading across the tile to the water fountain and a Pabst Blue Ribbon rolled down the hallway just as

Mr. Fowler, the assistant principal, rounded the corner.

DETENTION WAS ANY ROOM that wasn't being used over the lunch hour, and when all the cans had been stacked in Eddie's locker, Mr. Fowler marched Eddie, Dink, and Elizabeth to the first doorway they happened to come to. Inside, Miss Prendergast was correcting papers.

"These students are on detention for the remainder of activity period, Miss Prendergast," said the assistant principal. "Can you take them?"

The teacher looked up with a knotty frown forming between the eyebrows. "Take seats two rows apart," she instructed and, after Mr. Fowler had gone, she added, "I want *quiet*. I have twenty-eight papers to grade, and I've got to *think!*"

There were thirty-five minutes left to activity period, and Eddie knew there would be no lunch for them that day. He watched the red minute hand going around the clock above the door. He should have explained to Mr. Fowler. Instead, he had been trying to figure the number of cans and the number of pounds and had just divided and multiplied and was carrying a six when Mr. Fowler had appeared on the scene. Eddie had been so intent on keeping the figures in his head that he simply hadn't answered when Mr. Fowler asked what they thought they were doing. He was getting as bad as Joseph. And because Eddie hadn't said anything, Dink and Elizabeth hadn't tried to explain either. Partners stuck up for each other, always. But it was embarrassing for three bosses to be in detention.

Elizabeth was sitting with her chin in her hands. Every now and then her stomach rumbled and she shifted position. Dink had slipped one hand inside the desk where he was sitting and was slowly pulling out one thing after another to amuse himself.

Eddie watched him. Dink pulled out a yellow ballpoint pen and put it back. He pulled out some guitar strings and a tennis ball and put them back. Now and then Miss Prendergast looked up and Dink's hands froze inside the desk, but as soon as she went back to her papers, the pawing began again. Finally he pulled out a sandwich. He put his head down and sniffed it. Elizabeth covered her face with her hands.

Slowly, carefully, Dink set the sandwich in his lap and unwrapped it. Miss Prendergast looked up, and Dink looked out the window. Miss Prendergast looked down, and Dink lowered his head and took a bite.

Eddie tried to keep from laughing. Miss Prendergast looked up again. Dink's jaws stopped mov-

NIGHT DEPOSIT
BOX

ing. Miss Prendergast looked down, and Dink finished the sandwich.

THERE WERE OVER two-hundred beer cans in the collection, which helped. But no one brought any cans by on Tuesday or Wednesday. Janice Pringle and her brother brought a box on Thursday, but none came on Friday. On Saturday Dink went around the neighborhood with his garbage can carrier picking up stray cans, but the streets and alleys were surprisingly clean. He got nineteen cans and no more.

It was time, they concluded, to shut down. It was a corporate decision. No one wanted to wait around all day for one-and-a-half cents an hour. So the following Saturday they removed the rain gutter, shut the basement window, and painted "Going Out of Business" on the other side of the dart board.

And when they opened the night deposit box for the last time, they discovered that someone had put Mr. Clemmons' cat inside, and it was mad as anything.

FIVE

Losers

SUMMER. The Anselmino Aluminum Recycling Company had become the E.E.D. Lawn Mowing Company.

It wasn't the most original idea for a business, but other people had lawn mowing jobs, so Eddie decided that the three partners should try it. It was Elizabeth who put their initials together for a name.

The problem was that most of the neighborhood lawns were already signed up with somebody else. It made Eddie angry just to think about it. At the tender age of eleven, he already had to compete for a job. Wait till Herman the Terrible and the rest of the diaper gang were old enough to work!

"What you need is a gimmick," Roger said, sprawled on the glider where he was reading the Sunday paper. The business and financial sections were propped up on his stomach. "You have to convince people that the E.E.D. Lawn Mowing Company is different from Billy Watson's Lawn Mowing Service or Janice Pringle's Lawn Mowing Service. After all, why should they hire you instead of Janice or Billy if all the services are the same? You got me?"

"I think so," said Eddie.

"Look." Roger put down the business section and picked up an advertising supplement. " 'Harrigan's Restaurant, Where the Salad is Free!' That's a gimmick. Free salad means more customers, which means more money, which means that Harrigan can afford the free salad and still make a profit. Here's another one: 'Hillside Barbershop: Shoe Shine only fifteen cents with Every Haircut.' People want to feel as though they're getting something extra."

Eddie and his friends sat down in the back yard under the box elder and thought about it.

"We could lower our price and be the cheapest service in the neighborhood," said Dink.

"But we'd get less money," said Elizabeth. "We've got to buy gas, remember."

"We could offer to sweep off the walks and driveways afterwards," said Eddie.

"Janice Pringle already does that," said Dink.

"Maybe we could trim around all the trees with clippers," said Elizabeth.

"That's Billy Watson's gimmick," said Eddie.

Gloom settled down over them there in the

grass. The only sound was the tinkle of ice in their Seven-Up.

"Maybe we could do what my brother used to do," said Dink. "He had four other guys working with him, and they'd all go mow a lawn together."

"So who cares how we do it?" asked Elizabeth.

But Eddie saw the possibilities. "We can do it faster, that's why customers will care," he said. "Instead of annoying people with the noise of one lawn mower for an hour, we'll only annoy them for twenty minutes because we'll have three mowers going all at the same time. We can advertise, 'E.E.D. Lawn Mowing Company: Service in Triple Time.' "

Eddie paid Joseph a quarter to type up eight announcements on a single sheet of paper. On Monday he took the paper to the library and made seven copies on the Xerox machine for ten cents a copy. The E.E.D. Lawn Mowing Company had already gone ninety-five cents in the hole, including the payment to Joseph.

On Monday afternoon, Eddie, Dink, and Elizabeth cut the papers into 56 separate announcements and went around the neighborhood dropping them into the mail boxes of all the houses within two blocks.

"If even half of the fifty-six people hire you," Joseph, the Walking Calculator, said, "at four dollars per yard you'll earn one hundred and twelve dollars, divided by three is about thirty-seven dollars apiece, and if you invest at five and a half per- cent . . ."

THE FIRST CALL came on Thursday. The woman was a little nervous about having three lawn mowers all going in her yard at the same time, especially be- cause there was a newborn baby next door, but since Eddie's company would do the mowing three times as fast, she thought perhaps it was worth trying.

Eddie, Dink, and Elizabeth arrived promptly at one o'clock. Mrs. Gallagher gave them careful in- structions about the flowers, which weren't to be cut, and the bushes, which weren't to be trampled, and the dogwood tree, which was not to be bumped. Then the three machines started up.

It *was* a terrible racket. Eddie hadn't realized how awful three lawn mowers at once could be. But the most awful thing was that the E.E.D. Lawn Mowing Company was through before it really got started.

Dink was doing the back yard, Elizabeth was mowing the side yard, and Eddie was taking the front. Both Eddie and Elizabeth had seen the woman next door looking anxiously out of her window, and both of them knew that she was trying to get her newborn baby to sleep, so both were hurrying just a little faster. Elizabeth was just coming around the pine tree on the corner from the side and Eddie was coming around it from in front, when the Toro and the Tecumseh collided.

Ker-bang! Whang! Whaaaazzzz!

The Tecumseh climbed on top of the Toro and was chewing up a nut and bolt. Before either Elizabeth or Eddie could turn them off, the two machines had lurched forward in tandem and knocked over the prize rosebush. By the time the engines were stopped, a piece of the Toro was lying in the grass. There was no sound but the drone of Dink's machine coming from the backyard and the wail of the baby next door. Mrs. Gallagher came rushing down the front steps and stared speechless at her once-beautiful rosebush.

By Friday word had traveled about the neighborhood, and the few customers who had already made appointments called to cancel. It was just as well. The Toro wouldn't run at all until it had a new nut and bolt, and on Friday afternoon Eddie took his allowance and went to the hardware store.

HE STOOD THERE with the chewed-up metal in his hand. All the way to the shopping center, his bike had seemed to be squeaking:

Loser, loser,
Eddie is a loser.

Okay, it was true. He'd never be a business-man. So everyone else in the family was successful at something except him—the peewee, the runt, the nitwit, the shrimp . . .

He'd tried two jobs already, and neither had worked out. He'd embarrassed himself in front of family, friends, and neighbors, and twice was enough.

Okay, so he wouldn't make any money. He wouldn't have a job. He'd lie around all summer and watch TV and be bored, that's what. He'd grow up to be a bum. His father would have to hire him in the produce store because nobody else would want a loser.

Old Mr. Lowry was looking at the remains of the nut and bolt in Eddie's hand. He picked them up and examined them through his thick glasses.

"Well, now, I've got that size here someplace," he said as he shuffled off to the long row of little boxes on one side of the store. "Might take me awhile, but I've got 'em."

Eddie sauntered around with his hands in his pockets, looking at all the gadgets. Somewhere, somehow, somebody had come up with the idea for every one of them. Like Mr. Clemmons in his workshop, there were inventors for each item in Mr. Lowry's store. Like Mr. Clemmons, they had probably spent weeks or months or years working on some small thing that would eventually be in all the hardware stores. And, like Mr. Clemmons, they had all started with a problem.

He was walking by the plumbing supplies—the bath plugs and chains and faucets and soap dishes—when something caught his eye and he stopped. There, in a cardboard box, were some little plastic see-through packages. In each package were two rolled-up wire sacks, along with a metal clip. Up at the top of the display, printed on the cardboard, were the words, "Lint Trap."

Eddie stared at one of the packages. Mr. Clemmons' name wasn't on it anywhere, and he had a sickening feeling in the pit of his stomach. When he paid for the nut and bolt, he spent the rest of his allowance on the Lint Trap.

"Just got those in," Mr. Lowry said as he dropped it in the sack. "Selling like wild fire. All the women want one."

Slowly Eddie rode home and went over to Mr. Clemmons' workshop.

"Hey, Eddie, just in time!" the baldheaded man said. "Look at this!"

Eddie didn't want to look, but he had to. Mr. Clemmons was holding the gallon jar upside down, and water was gushing through the hose and out through the wire cage. The string and hair and fuzz and lint all stayed behind in the cage this time. The water in the basin was sparkling clean.

"I did it!" said Mr. Clemmons. "I made the cage of finer mesh, and it traps it all. Now I just have to figure out a simple way to hold it onto the hose."

Eddie couldn't say anything. He felt as though he were going to throw up, and Mr. Clemmons noticed.

"Hey, what's wrong?" he asked, coming over. "Something the matter, Eddie?"

Eddie stuck his hand in his pocket and pulled out the Lint Trap. He handed it to Mr. Clemmons.

For a long time the tall man stared at the package without blinking. His face looked like stone. He did not even seem to be breathing. Finally he turned it over, saw the directions on the back, but did not read them. Without a word, he slipped the package in his pocket and walked slowly toward the house.

SIX

Pigfoot

JULY WAS EVEN MORE BORING than June. Eddie had absolutely nothing to do. Mr. Anselmino went to work early every morning because the fresh fruit arrived about seven. Mrs. Anselmino made preserves each day on the big table in the kitchen, and Roger was getting ready for the annual shoe sale, the Midsummer Extravaganza. Even Joseph had somewhere to go. He was enrolled in a summer school class for gifted children, called "Exploring Business Careers."

Eddie stayed in bed as long as he could every morning—at least until Roger and Joseph were out of the house. Then he slipped down to the kitchen, smeared some hot preserves on a piece of bread and butter, and watched the stupid television.

He started with the kiddie cartoons and "Sesame Street," worked his way through the game shows, the news at noon, and finally into the afternoon soap operas.

He really didn't care for any of it, but the soap operas were the worst. Laura loved Frank who was dying, and the doctor who performed the operation was upset because his only daughter had a car accident when she was leaving home to live with a shoplifter, but the judge was lenient because she reminded him of an adopted daughter who had run away with a house painter.

It was almost a relief when the commercials came on and a woman talked about denture breath or floor wax or vitamins. And seven minutes later she was back again talking about ring-around-the-collar. At least Eddie thought it was the same woman. After awhile all the women looked alike to him—just as bored and colorless as he felt inside.

He couldn't even go to see Mr. Clemmons because the inventor hadn't been back to his workshop since the day Eddie had given him the Lint Trap. Elizabeth had gone to Delaware on vacation, and Dink had gone to Michigan. Because Eddie was bored, he was irritable. And when he was irritable, he seemed to get in everybody's way. All day he walked back and forth to the television set changing channels, up and down the stairs to change from a long-sleeved shirt to a short-sleeved shirt to a tank top; back and forth to the telephone to see if Dink or Elizabeth had come home early; in and out of the house to see if the ice cream truck was coming; and back and forth to the window to see if Mr. Clemmons was in his shop yet.

"For goodness sake, can't you stay put?" his mother would say.

And things had gotten particularly bad between Eddie and Joseph. Every morning, when Joseph went off to class, he would stumble over a pair of Eddie's sneakers, left by the front door. Every morning Joseph would bellow, "Would somebody please ask Eddie to pick up his stinking shoes?" And Eddie would pick them up, but often they didn't get further than the upstairs hallway, and then Joseph would stumble over them again when he got home.

THE OTHER TROUBLE between them was that Joseph said that Eddie stank. Whenever Joseph picked up Eddie's sneakers himself, he held them out at arm's length and wrinkled up his nose. Whenever he found Eddie's socks in a heap in the bathroom, he would throw them out in the hall as far as they would go.

Eddie didn't think his feet were so unusual. It was only when he sniffed at Joseph's socks once that he realized *some* people's feet smelled like soap and cotton, and *some* people's feet smelled like garbage.

And then one afternoon when all the windows had been closed in Eddie's room and his bed was unmade and his pajamas were lying about and there was a heap of dirty socks in one corner, Joseph came up to call Eddie to dinner.

As soon as he opened the door, he began gasping: "Arrrggg! This place smells like a pigpen! Give me a gas mask, somebody, quick!"

Eddie thought about it at dinner that night, scowling at everybody, daring anybody to speak to him. Smelly feet were busy feet, that's all. Feet that were going back and forth to the window and the phone and the television all day were bound to be sweaty, no question about it. It was quiet, stuck-up feet like Joseph's that smelled like soap and cotton.

Or maybe Eddie's feet smelled because they were sad feet. Feet that were unloading a produce truck or setting up a window display or walking back and forth to summer school for gifted children were happy feet. It was only feet that were inside all day, when they'd rather be out building bridges or something, that stunk up the house.

"Hey, Pigfoot," Joseph said just before he went to bed that night. "Pick up your shoes, will you, so I won't have to smell them outside my door all night?"

What Joseph needed was a punch in the mouth, but Eddie suddenly had an idea. If there were two smelly feet, there had to be four, and if there were four, there were probably twenty or thirty or forty. He couldn't be the only kid in Detroit whose feet were offensive.

Find a problem, Mr. Clemmons had said, *and you've got yourself a business.*

THE NEXT MORNING after his father and brothers had left the house, Eddie went to his mother and asked if she had any cologne she didn't want any more.

Mrs. Anselmino was mixing a batch of banana bread on the table and listening to an opera on the kitchen radio.

"On my dresser," she instructed, in rhythm with the mixing spoon, "in the yellow glass bottle," and she went on humming Verdi.

Eddie found the bottle and took it into his room with a box of gauze pads from the medicine chest.

Pigfoot—The Answer to Smelly Feet.

It was a marvelous trade name, a fantastic gimmick. When he made his first five thousand dollars, he might even give a percentage to Joseph just for the idea. This time, however, the business was all

his. He wouldn't even tell Dink and Elizabeth about it. He'd be the one and only boss.

Carefully, he soaked two of the gauze pads with "Dew of Roses." Then he took his sneakers off and placed a pad in each one.

It was a little difficult getting used to them under his feet, but after walking up and down the stairs several dozen times, the gauze flattened out. All he could feel was something damp soaking up through his socks, and he knew that Pigfoot was doing its job.

He straightened his room, hung up his clothes, made his bed, and then sat down on the floor to work out some advertising slogans.

"Big Foot? Try Pigfoot, the Deodorant for Oversized Feet!"

"Pigfoot—the Shoe Deodorizer for People who Perspire."

He got out his old notebook, tore out the sheet that said Anselmino Aluminum Recycling Company, and wrote, "Pigfoot Associates." There weren't any associates, of course, but he liked the sound of it. And maybe, if the company was successful, he'd let Dink and Elizabeth in on it later.

After that he got a piece of poster board and drew his first advertisement. It was a picture of a pig with wavy lines coming up from his feet to show that they smelled bad. With a magic marker, he printed at the top:

Smelly Feet?

And then, under the picture:

*Try Pigfoot, for Pigs Who Want to
Smell Like People.*

He loved it. The pig had a sort of strange smile on its face—in fact, it looked a lot like Herman the Terrible, but its feet and tail were good, and besides, the message was the main thing.

After dinner, Eddie worked for several hours in his room making more packets of Pigfoot. After saturating each piece of gauze, he folded plastic wrap around it so that it wouldn't dry out, and put it in a cigar box with the others. Tomorrow he would take the box over to the drugstore and ask Mr. Perona if he would sell them for twenty-five cents each.

ABOUT NINE O'CLOCK that evening, he went down in the living room to test his product. Roger was listening to a record and waving a finger back and forth in time to the music. Mrs. Anselmino was sitting at the dining room table writing a letter to her sister, and Joseph was playing poker with his father. Joseph, the Boy Wonder, had fourteen red chips in front of him; Mr. Anselmino had only two.

Eddie sat down on the couch beside Roger. Nobody paid any attention to him. After a while he stretched out his legs and began wiggling his feet in time to the music. Still no one responded. So far so good. No odor yet. Now for the acid test.

Eddie took off his sneakers and put his feet up on the coffee table.

A moment later Mrs. Anselmino raised her head. She sniffed the air, frowned, and went back to her letter.

Roger looked around. "Hey, Mom, you got anything on the stove?" he asked.

But before she could answer, Joseph let out a gasp. "Yuk! What's that awful smell? Open the doors! Open the windows!" He clutched dramatically at his throat.

Mr. Anselmino got up and opened the door. A draft blew across Eddie's feet and sneakers and came curling up to his nose.

He had never smelled such an odor in his life. It smelled like burning rubber and rotten rose petals and sweaty feet. It smelled like mildewed potatoes and fermented sugar and old tee-shirts.

"It's Pigfoot again!" Joseph bellowed. "Somebody make him take a bath! Somebody throw his sneakers out! Somebody wash his socks! Awwwkkk! I can't stand it!"

Eddie picked up his shoes and ran upstairs. He took the packets of cologne from his sneakers, put his socks in the hamper, and locked himself in the bathroom. For an hour he soaked in the tub, humiliated. When he came out, his skin was as wrinkled as a raisin. The bottoms of his feet were all white and soggy and had started to peel around the heels.

"Are you all right, Eddie?" called his father from below.

"Yeah."

He went into his room and stared at the Pigfoot advertisement. It had seemed like such a good idea. Slowly he picked up the magic marker and drew a big X across it. Then he tore another page out of his notebook. As he turned to throw it into the wastebasket, he noticed a can of foot powder on his dresser. His mother must have set it there. In big words on the front of the can it said that all you had to do was shake some in each shoe and you'd never be offensive again.

He didn't even touch the can. He didn't want to read any more about it. He knew exactly how Mr.

Clemmons had felt when he discovered that his invention had already been invented.

Eddie took the cigar box into the bathroom and flushed all the Pigfoot packets down the toilet.

SEVEN

South End Weekly

WHAT FINALLY TOOK Eddie away from "All My Children" and "Search for Tomorrow" was the return of Dink and Elizabeth.

It was Elizabeth who had the idea this time. She said that at the beach where she stayed, somebody had printed up a weekly newsletter. It told what shows were going on in town; described a restaurant or two; published news about local residents; and carried a few ads for swim supplies and pet food. Why not publish a one-page newspaper for their neighborhood, she suggested, called *The South End Weekly?*

An idea always seemed more exciting to Eddie when he thought it up himself, but he couldn't afford to be choosy. He was glad to have his partners back again, glad he didn't have to tell them about Pigfoot. He said he'd ask Joseph to type up their paper.

The first problem, of course, was that he and

Joseph were barely speaking these days. The second was that they would need not just one paper typed, but dozens.

"Joseph could make carbon copies," said Dink.

They divided up the jobs; Dink was to be the advertising manager, Elizabeth was news editor, and Eddie—because of his relationship to Joseph, the typist, upon whom it all depended—was named editor-in-chief.

Eddie was especially careful to pick up his sneakers for the next day or two and not leave them lying about where Joseph could stumble over them. When Joseph talked at the table about his final exam in summer school and how he was the only one to get thirty-nine out of forty questions right, Eddie listened politely. And finally, when Joseph went to the pool one day and asked to borrow Eddie's goggles, Eddie said "Sure," and after that they were speaking again.

As a matter of fact, when Eddie finally asked Joseph if he would type up the newspaper for them, Joseph said he would type the first edition free because he didn't have anything else to do.

THE *South End Weekly* held a staff conference on Thursday in Eddie's basement where the Anselmino Aluminum Recycling Company had once been. They sat around the card table with their notebooks and pencils and counted up the want ads and news items they had collected so far.

Dink had gone from house to house selling advertising space for a nickel and had sold four ads for lost pets, nine ads for baby sitters needed, two ads for music lessons, and one ad for a 1971 Buick. They felt especially good about the Buick. There was big money, Dink said, in cars.

Elizabeth had spent four days trudging about the neighborhood with her notebook looking for news items. She had written an article about the twenty-fifth anniversary of Mr. Perona's drugstore, an item about Mrs. Sebert's gall bladder operation, an announcement of the new baby next to Mrs. Gallagher's house, a report of the trash fire behind the Lowry Hardware store, birthday greetings to Herman the Terrible who was now one year old, and finally, a feature story on ways to keep cool in August.

It had looked like a lot of writing—four notebook pages—but once it was typed, it filled only one page with an inch at the end to spare. Eddie used the last inch for this announcement:

The South End Weekly
Subscribe Today!
Only 15¢ a copy!

There was a problem, however. Joseph could only make four copies at a time, and he had only offered to type one page, not dozens. Also, his typing wasn't perfect, and though he corrected all the mistakes on the original, the carbon copies had big black smudges on them and had to be thrown out. There was nothing to do but make copies on the machine at the library for ten cents each.

"We'll still make a five cent profit on each one," said Dink. "And we've got sixteen ads at a nickel apiece, so we've got eighty cents to start with."

It was decided that they would use the eighty cents to make eight copies. When those sold, they would have one dollar and twenty cents, and could make twelve more copies. When those sold, they would have one dollar and eighty cents and could make eighteen copies. They wouldn't be losing any money as long as they didn't spend more than they made.

It was, Eddie thought, the best business they'd had so far. They began early Saturday morning, and by three o'clock, had been to the library four times to make copies. On the fourth trip, they made twenty-seven copies.

"Hey, hold on," said Dink. "We're spending all

the profits. Somewhere we've got to stop and keep the money."

They held another conference. The first eight copies had sold immediately to their own families. Mrs. Anselmino even bought several extras to send to relatives. The next twelve copies had also sold well, mostly to the people who had placed the want ads. When they made the third batch, the eighteen copies had gone a little more slowly. Now they had twenty-seven papers. It seemed like a good time to stop.

"Okay, this is it," said Eddie. "Whatever money we make this time, we keep."

It was more difficult than they'd thought. People who didn't know them at all said "no." Some simply closed the door without finding out what it was they were selling. It didn't help, either, that Janice Pringle's brother followed them around with a copy of their paper making fun of Joseph's spelling. (Joseph may have been a brain at math, but he was terrible at spelling.)

Nevertheless, by eight that evening, the last of the twenty-seven copies had been sold, making a grand profit of four dollars and five cents. After keeping out one dollar and five cents to begin on the next Saturday, Eddie, Dink and Elizabeth each received one dollar.

It wasn't bad, but it wasn't exactly good, either. They had worked a whole week for that money. Joseph would not do any more typing free, and they would have to pay him *fifty* cents, he had said, to type any more. Still, it had been a small success, and Mr. Anselmino said that most businesses didn't make a profit in their first year. If Eddie was ever to become a businessman, he'd have to be patient.

At the end of the second Saturday, Eddie, Dink, and Elizabeth were left with eleven unsold copies. After paying Joseph, their profit was only fifty-five cents each. They knew that the third week would be even more difficult. Even the people who were looking for babysitters were complaining because there were far more children needing to be sat than there were who were willing to do the sitting.

THE LAST STAFF CONFERENCE of *The South End Weekly* took place in Eddie's basement that night, and it was unanimously decided to shut down. The newspaper wasn't a failure; it just seemed to make good sense to quit while they were ahead.

But it didn't make Eddie feel any better about himself or his business career. Somewhere there just had to be a job that was simple, easy, and where nobody told you what to do. He just hadn't found it yet.

The only thing nice that had happened was

that Mr. Clemmons was out in his workshop again.

Eddie went over to see him.

"I've got an idea, Eddie," Mr. Clemmons said, and he looked happy again. He held up the two Lint Traps that had come in the package Eddie had given him. One was full of lint and fuzz and hair and string, and the other was empty.

"Look at this," Mr. Clemmons went on. "I've been using the Lint Trap on my washing machine, and of course it works very well—much better than mine. But see? Once it fills up with lint, you have to throw it away. It's impossible to get the stuff out of the wire. And when the second bag gets gukked up, you have to go back to the store and buy another package for one dollar and seventy-nine cents. Right? Right."

He reached into his pocket and took out something that looked like a hair net. He slipped it down inside the unused Lint Trap like the lining of a glove.

"I'm working on a Lint Trap Liner, you see, that only costs a few pennies. A woman could buy a whole box of Lint Trap Liners and throw one away after each wash. If one ever broke open, the Lint Trap would still hold the stuff so that it couldn't go down the drain. I'm going to get a patent on this and then go see the people who make Lint Traps. I'll sell them my idea."

"Hey, Mr. Clemmons, that's really great!" Eddie told him.

"Where there's a problem, there's a business," said Mr. Clemmons. "Don't you ever forget it."

EIGHT

Sixth Grade Sing Day

By the time school began again in September, Eddie had another idea. It was a great idea about something awful.

Ever since the South End Middle School had opened, there had been a tradition. In September, there was always a pep rally where the sixth graders were introduced to the school song, which they were supposed to learn before the first big basketball game in October. It was expected that all the sixth graders would come to the game prepared to sing their lungs out, and boost the team to victory. And to this end, the awful, terrible tradition known as Sixth-Grade Sing Day had begun.

At the pep rally, the sixth graders were told to memorize the song. They were told to attend the big game. And they were warned that a week before the game, a certain day would be set aside for Sixth-Grade Sing Day. On this dreadful day, any seventh

or eighth grader could stop a sixth grader in the hall and demand that he sing the school song. If he could not, the rumor went, he would be dunked in the drinking fountain, thrown in the showers, or have spaghetti dumped over his head in the school cafeteria. (As if having to sing a solo in front of the upper classmen were not torture enough.)

Eddie had been through Sixth-Grade Sing Day the year before. He had gone to school with his knees knocking, his mouth dry, his hands sweaty, and had been backed up against the wall four times between classes and asked to sing. Dink, who could never carry a tune, had tried valiantly to sing when he was asked, but no one liked the sound of it very much, so he had been dunked in the drinking fountain anyway. And Elizabeth had been so terrified that she had hid under the bleachers at lunch time and spent the whole afternoon in the gym.

No one was sure just why Sixth-Grade Sing Day continued. Each year the Student Council voted to keep it going because they always took the vote after the dreadful day was over, and then the sixth graders knew they could do it the next year to somebody else. But every year, the incoming sixth graders awaited the day with horror and dread, and Eddie could still remember the awfulness of it.

*   *   *

It was on the bus to school the first day of seventh grade that the idea came to him: SPCSG, or Society for the Prevention of Cruelty to Sixth Graders. Not only did Dink and Elizabeth think it was a great idea, but Janice Pringle, her brother Tom, and Billy Watson did as well.

For the next few weeks, the six of them—the charter members of SPCSG—talked to all the sixth graders they could find about Sixth-Grade Sing Day. They told them that for twenty five cents they could buy themselves a little protection. Everyone who paid up was put on a list and told to meet Eddie outside the main door before school on the big day.

It came at last, and even the sky looked mean and angry, as though it were in on the plot. Sixty-one terrified sixth graders were waiting for Eddie at the front door when he arrived with his roster of names. He read them one by one, and as they went into the school, Elizabeth gave them each a green rubber band to wear on their wrists. Whenever a seventh or eighth grader stopped them, Dink said, they were to hold their hands up high in the air and one of the six SPCSG members would come to their aid.

Eddie, Dink, and Elizabeth were to take the second floor; Janice, Tom, and Billy would take the first. Whenever a sixth grader was trapped, an SPCSG person was to come running and sing the song with him as loudly as he or she could. No one could stop the upper classmen from demanding that the sixth graders sing, of course, but there was no rule against somebody singing along, which took away some of the embarrassment. In fact, if anybody heard Dink singing, he might just call off the whole thing.

By the time the last sixth grader was in the building, Eddie could already hear the signs of torture going on. He and Dink and Elizabeth rushed up to the second floor where a small sixth grader was backed up against the lockers, and some eighth-grade boys were shouting, "Come on, man, sing it with feeling!" Every time little Charlie Evans opened his mouth, only a terrified wheeze came out.

Eddie saw the green rubber band on Charlie's wrist and lunged through the crowd. "Come on, Charlie," he said. "We'll sing a duet!" And he began belting out the old school song:

> *South End Middle School,*
> *That's our name.*
> *We've got spirit!*
> *We've got fame!*
> *Come on, boys,*
> *And show your might!*

Knock'em down and
Win this fight!

By the time the song was finished, little Charlie was actually smiling; he almost enjoyed it. The eighth grade boys were disappointed and slunk away, eager to find somebody else who hadn't yet reached the safety of a classroom.

ALL DAY Eddie, Dink, and Elizabeth worked as fast as they could on the second floor, while Janice, Tom, and Billy took care of the first. All over the place sixth graders were being stopped; in the halls, on the basketball court, beneath the flag pole, and under the clock. They were being forced to sing in the cafeteria and the auditorium and the locker rooms.

But whenever a hand with a green rubber band around the wrist went up, an SPCSG member was there. Whenever there was the sound of timid bleating and croaking from somebody on the roster, an SPCSG member was on the spot to help out.

Eddie, Dink, Elizabeth, Janice, Tom and Billy weren't very popular around school that day, of course, except with the sixth graders, who worshipped them; and at one point Billy Watson got thrown in the showers. But a job was a job, and most of the seventh and eighth graders wished they'd thought up the SPCSG themselves.

By three o'clock, only one person who had signed up with the SPCSG had had to sing the song alone and that was because he had been trapped in the toilets, so Eddie gave him his money back.

Still, sixty sixth graders had paid twenty-five cents, which came to fifteen dollars, and that, divided between six people, was two dollars and fifty cents apiece. Not bad for a day's work.

Eddie was just about to board the bus for home when a big hand closed over his arm, and the next thing he knew he was being ushered into Mr. Fowler's office.

Mr. Fowler sat down on the edge of his desk and motioned Eddie to a chair.

"It was reported to me this afternoon by several different students that you are running a protection racket of some kind, Eddie," he said. "What's this all about?"

A protection racket? Somehow that didn't sound so good.

"I've been told," Mr. Fowler went on, "that you've been extorting money from some of the younger students."

Extorting? That was a word Eddie didn't know,

but it didn't sound so good either.

Mr. Fowler picked up a paper clip and kept dropping it back and forth from one hand to the other. "Is all this true, Eddie?"

"I guess so," said Eddie.

"You've been collecting twenty-five cents from the younger kids?"

"Yes."

"With promises of protection if they paid?"

"Yes."

"How many students did you collect from?"

"Sixty-one, but Johnny Goldstein got trapped in the toilets, so I gave him his money back."

"What do you mean, he got trapped in the toilets? What happened to him? What happens to kids who don't pay up?" Mr. Fowler looked positively fierce.

Eddie shrugged. "They sing alone."

"Sing?"

"Yeah, you know—Sixth-Grade Sing Day."

The paper clip fell to the floor. Mr. Fowler rubbed one hand across his face as though he were trying to wipe away a smile, but it came anyway. "You mean that's what it was all about—Sixth Grade Sing Day?"

"Yeah. Anybody who paid got help with the singing. We just tried to make it a little less embarrassing for them, that's all."

"Well, I don't know, Eddie," the vice-principal said, but he was smiling broadly now. "It still sounds like a racket to me."

"And it seems to *me*," said Eddie, "that if there weren't anything to protect the sixth graders *from*, there wouldn't have to be a racket."

"You're absolutely right," said Mr. Fowler, and he stood up. "It's all supposed to be done in the name of school spirit, but it does get out of hand. I think maybe you and your friends showed the most school spirit of all in your concern for the incoming class. Come on, you've missed your bus. I'll drive you home."

Because they came to Mr. Anselmino's produce store first, Eddie asked to be let off there, and Mr. Fowler insisted on coming in and telling the whole story to Eddie's father over the rutabagas and onions.

AT DINNER THAT NIGHT, Mr. Anselmino looked proudly at Eddie and bragged about what Mr. Fowler had said. Eddie had to tell the story all over again for the whole family, and even Joseph was impressed.

"That's my boy; always thoughtful of others," said Mrs. Anselmino.

"Good show, Eddie!" said Roger.

"Wow! Two dollars and fifty cents at five and a half percent!" said Joseph.

It was nice while it lasted, but unfortunately it was over. Kaput. Finished. A one-time show. What Eddie wanted was a job that lasted all year. He wanted a desk with a telephone on it, a rubber stamp with his name on it, a book for expenses, and a box for cash receipts.

And just after he went to bed that night, the idea came to him; just when he had his mind on other things, it slipped into his head so quietly he hardly knew it was there. Just when he was about to give up, the problem came to him. He sat up in bed and yelled at the top of his lungs:

"Eureka!"

NINE

Eddie, Incorporated

AT BREAKFAST the next morning, he made his announcement.

"I've found it!" he said. "I've found a problem!"

"I thought you were looking for a job," said Joseph.

"Find a problem, and you've got yourself a business," Eddie told him. And then he explained his idea.

There were too many kids in South End, that's what. There might be a lot of sixth graders needing protection. But there were a whole lot more little kids. There were more and more tricycles to fall over on the sidewalk and more and more toddlers to hide in Mr. Anselmino's potato bin. Which meant that there were dozens and dozens of parents wanting to get away from it all for an evening or two, and dozens and dozens of babies that needed sitting. But

—as the want ads in the *South End Weekly* should have shown him—there weren't that many older children willing to sit them.

That was the problem.

"I'm going to run a sitting service," Eddie told his family. "I'm going to start an agency."

He watched for the faintest sign of a frown or a cough or a smirk, but there weren't any.

"I tell you what you need," said Roger. "A contract. You've got to have a contract. You've got to make it so the parents know what they're getting and the sitters know what to expect."

Mrs. Anselmino nodded. "And you've got to be reliable. You've got to have substitutes so that if one sitter can't make it, you'll have somebody to take his place."

"And decide on your fee," said Mr. Anselmino. "Either a percentage of the payment, or a flat fee."

Joseph was quiet for a moment. "I wish I'd thought of this," he said finally.

BUT EDDIE was one step ahead of them He was already working it out in his head, and by the time he called Dink and Elizabeth over, he knew just how it was going to be.

"When parents need a sitter," he explained, "they won't have to make seven or eight phone calls before they find one. All they'll have to do is call our agency, and we'll find the sitter for them."

"But hardly any of the kids at school want to sit," said Elizabeth.

"And some of the parents complain about the ones who do," said Dink.

"Exactly," said Eddie. "We've got to find out why and write up two contracts. Both sitters and parents will have to sign a contract before we take them on as clients."

Clients. Eddie loved the word. It slid off his tongue like a butter cream. *Clients. Contracts. Percentages. Profits.*

Eddie, Dink, and Elizabeth spent the first Saturday interviewing parents about what they expected of a sitter. They spent the second Saturday talking with their friends about what they expected on a job. Then they wrote up the two contracts:

I

A Sitter is expected to:
1. Be on time.
2. Avoid long conversations on the phone with friends.
3. Eat only what he has been told he can eat.

4. Give full attention to the child and not spend the evening in front of the TV.
5. Leave the house as he found it, without candy wrappers on the rug and Coke bottles on the piano.
6. Keep out of the parents' stuff.
7. Let the agency know as soon as possible if he can't sit as planned.

I understand that I am an employee of the agency, and I will pay 25¢ for each job that it gets for me. I also understand that if I fail to obey the rules of the contract, my name will be removed from their register.

Sitter's signature _____

The second contract read:

II

Parents are expected to:

1. Be home at the agreed time.
2. Require no housecleaning or dishwashing.
3. Leave a list of phone numbers in case of emergency.

4. Tell their kid that they are leaving and not just sneak out the door.
5. Drive the sitter home afterwards.
6. Pay the sitter $1 per hour, $2 after midnight.
7. Call the agency as soon as possible if they discover they will not be going out after all.

We understand that we are clients of the agency and will not contact agency sitters on our own. We will pay the agency 25¢ each time a sitter is provided for us, and we further understand that if we do not obey the rules of the contract, our name will be removed from the register.

Parents' signature _____

It took a long time to write the contracts. The wording had to be just right, and Mrs. Anselmino and Roger helped cross out and rewrite until everyone was satisfied that the contracts said what they were supposed to say.

"What will you do if a sitter gets sick at the last minute?" Elizabeth asked Eddie.

"We'll have a backup crew for emergencies."

"You don't mean . . . ?"

"You got it," said Eddie. "The three of us."

THE LAST THING they had to decide on was a name. Eddie thought that the E.E.D. Sitting Service was a good one; Dink liked the Acme Sitters Agency.

"We might even decide to expand," Eddie told them. "We could send a whole crew out to help with kids' birthday parties, for example. They could blow up the balloons, push the kids on the swings, help serve the ice cream and cake, mop up afterwards . . . Or maybe we could have a pet and plant sitting service too—like when people go on vacation and need somebody to feed the dog or water the plants while they're gone. Why, there's no end to the services we could provide."

Elizabeth was watching him from across the room. Her blue-tinted glasses were pushed up on her head, and she looked very thoughtful.

"You know," she said, "if it weren't for Eddie's ideas, we wouldn't even be having this conversation. We wouldn't even have the money to make copies of the contracts. We're all partners, I know, but it's really Eddie's business, and I think we should call it 'Eddie, Incorporated,' because nobody knows what he'll think of next. Whatever it is, the name will fit."

So Eddie, Incorporated it was, and the name and phone number went at the top of both contracts.

Between them, they had seven dollars and fifty cents from Sixth-Grade Sing Day. They gave the fifty cents to Joseph to type up the contracts, and used the seven dollars to make seventy copies of them—thirty-five of each.

As the papers piled up higher and higher on the copying machine at the library, people began coming over to see what was going on.

"Now what are you up to?" said the head librarian, and she read copies of the contracts. "Say, this sounds pretty good! Why don't you tack an announcement up on our community bulletin board?"

Parents stopped by and looked over the contracts as the stack of papers grew even higher.

"How can we sign up for this?" they wanted to know.

Elizabeth took down their names as Dink went back and forth to the desk for change and Eddie continued to run off copies. They had eleven names before they even left the library.

That afternoon they began a tour of the neighborhood, knocking on doors and explaining the contracts.

"Does it cost anything to register with you?" people wanted to know.

"Only a dime to pay for the contract," Eddie would tell them, and if they were interested, they would sign it, with Eddie as a witness. Then he would write down their name, address, and phone number on his roster. Even the parents of Herman the Terrible—the big bad baby over on Locust Street—signed up. Parents of toddlers, parents of twins—they all wanted their names on the register.

Meanwhile Dink and Elizabeth were going around to the homes of their friends, explaining the service to them. By seven that evening, when they met once more at the mailbox on the corner, Eddie had the names of twenty-two parents and Dink and Elizabeth had fourteen sitters. Each had paid a dime for the contract, so there was already three dollars and sixty cents in the cash box. And when they finally got back to Eddie's house, Mrs. Anselmino was waiting for them on the porch.

"The phone's been ringing all afternoon," she said. "I've got nine parents who want a sitter for next Saturday night, and I told them you'd call back."

THE BUSINESS GREW STEADILY. Each week there were more calls from people who had seen the announcement at the library or who had heard about Eddie, Incorporated from someone else.

As soon as a call came in, Eddie would take down the information and begin calling his list of sitters to see who could take the job. He would call the parents back to tell them whom to expect, and then the name would be written down in his notebook. When the sitting job was over, Dink would go collect a quarter from the parents the next morning, and Elizabeth would collect a quarter from the sitter. The fifty cents would go into the cash box in Eddie's basement, and at the end of each week, they would divide the money between them.

The first week they made about seven dollars altogether, and the next week nine. Sometimes there would be a little less money, sometimes a little more, and sometimes they would have to use some of the profits to make more copies of the contracts. But they always made a profit. They could always count on something. It was a steady business they could depend on, and growing every week. Already parents were asking for sitters for New Year's Eve, and one woman wanted to know if the agency would feed her goldfish when she went to Florida over Christmas.

Parents liked the agency because they did not have to worry that their sitter might get sick at the last minute and ruin their plans. They knew that if that happened, the agency would send somebody else.

Sitters liked the agency because they knew that if a big party came up suddenly and they had already promised to babysit, the agency would find someone to take their place. Both parents and sitters liked the agency because they knew that the other person had read the contract and would obey the rules.

Occasionally a sitter's name was removed from the register because there seemed to be too many parties and the sitter was never available. And sometimes parents were taken off the list because they continued to come home much later than they had promised. But not only was Eddie, Incorporated successful, it was becoming well known in the neighborhood.

In fact, Eddie had been so busy making phone calls that he almost forgot his own birthday. It wasn't until he saw the three-layer cake on the table one night in November that he realized he was now twelve.

The family had not forgotten, however. As butter pecan ice cream dribbled off Eddie's chin and he stuffed the last bite of fudge cake in his mouth, his mother pushed a present across the table toward him. "Open it, Eddie," she said. "I can't wait any longer."

Off came the red and white ribbons and inside was an engagement calendar for the coming year. Every day had its own page with lines for job assignments and telephone numbers. On the front was a photograph of a flock of geese flying south against a winter sunset. It looked very much like the calendar on Mr. Fowler's desk at school.

"This is great, Mom!" Eddie said delightedly. "I really mean it."

Mr. Anselmino's gift was next. It was a cloth-bound record book with blue columns for income and red columns for expenses, just like the one at the Anselmino Produce Store.

"I love it!" said Eddie.

"My present is sort of a surprise," said Roger. "You've got to go down in the basement to see it."

So Eddie, with his family trailing behind him, went down the basement stairs. There, on the card table desk, was a bright orange extension phone.

"Oh, wow!" Eddie yelled. "I can't believe this! I can't!"

Roger was smiling broadly. "Well, it was a little more than I'd planned to spend, but I got a raise last week, so I thought, 'What the heck.' "

Eddie stood and stared. They knew now that he wasn't just playing. Nobody had his own extension phone just to mess around. Nobody had an engagement calendar for the coming year if he was expected to go out of business in a week. Nobody had a record book for expenses if he hardly made any money worth recording.

And then he remembered Joseph. Joseph hadn't come down to the basement with them. He hadn't even wished Eddie a happy birthday. In fact, as soon as the cake and ice cream had been served, Joseph had disappeared.

Maybe Eddie would never be successful as far as Joseph was concerned. Maybe he'd always be Pigfoot to his brother, the Brain. Maybe Joseph thought it was all a dumb idea and didn't want to laugh in Eddie's face.

But just then Joseph came rushing breathlessly down the basement stairs and thrust something in Eddie's hand. "I forgot to wrap it," he explained. "Sorry about the homemade card, too, but I didn't have a chance to buy one."

Eddie unfolded the card. Joseph had taken an old snapshot of Eddie and cut out his face. He'd pasted the face on a sheet of paper and then drawn Eddie's body in a business suit, sitting at a desk with a telephone in his hand. Underneath the drawing Joseph had written, "Happy Birthday to the Big Wheel."

Eddie gulped. He wasn't Pigfoot any longer. He'd graduated.

He shook the package. It was very small, very light, and for a moment, Eddie was afraid it was going to be a dumb joke—a wheel off one of his old toy trucks or something. But inside the box was a rubber stamp, and on one side were the words, "Eddie, Incorporated."

Twelve was the best time in the whole world to be alive, Eddie decided. He couldn't wait to show his presents to Dink and Elizabeth. He couldn't wait to go next door and share a piece of his cake with Mr. Clemmons. He wanted to do everything at once —talk about income tax with his parents, advertising with Roger, and investments with Joseph.

But just at that moment the bright orange telephone rang on Eddie's desk, and he answered it.

"Eddie, Incorporated," he said.

It was Janice Pringle, and her voice sounded pitifully weak. "I'm supposed to sit for the O'Conners tonight, but I think I'm catching the flu," she said. "I just can't make it."

"Don't worry," Eddie told her. "I'll find somebody else."

He hung up. It wouldn't be easy. Elizabeth was out of town on a basketball trip. Dink was at a roller skating party. Most of the other sitters were already signed up for tonight, but somebody was expected to sit with Herman the Terrible in an hour. The par-

ents were on the register, and Eddie couldn't let them down, not even on his birthday. Business was business.

"Tell Mr. Clemmons I'll be over tomorrow with a slice of my cake," he told his family. And then, with a book for himself and a box of animal crackers for Herman, Eddie put on his jacket and went to work.

TEN

On the Job

HERMAN THE TERRIBLE was sitting by the living room window, his nose pressed against the glass. There was a dirty smudge on the pane. His eyes rolled to the left and watched as Eddie came up the steps and rang the bell.

Mr. and Mrs. O'Conner had their coats on, ready to leave.

"You're right on time," said Mrs. O'Conner. "Herman had a very late nap today, so I haven't given him his supper yet. You'll find it in the kitchen. And I'm afraid he won't be sleepy till around ten o'clock. You can manage, can't you?"

"Of course," said Eddie, wondering if he sounded sincere. But he was, after all, the head of the agency, the Sitter Supreme.

As soon as the parents had gone, Herman crawled over to where Eddie stood and sat looking at his ankle as though he might bite it.

"Hi," said Eddie.

Herman said nothing.

Eddie picked up the strong baby and took him out to the kitchen.

"Is that your supper?" Eddie asked, pointing to the jar of strained beets.

No answer. A dollop of drool trickled down Herman's chin and onto his bib.

Eddie set Herman in his high chair. "Okay, kid," he said. "I'm the new cafeteria manager around here." He dipped the spoon into the jar and held it in front of Herman, waiting for him to open his mouth.

"Yum, yum," said Eddie. "Good strained beets. Delicious, nutritious red beets."

Herman's mouth remained closed. How did mothers ever get food into their babies, anyway? Eddie wondered. Pour it in their ears?

At that moment the spoon accidentally touched Herman's lower lip, and his mouth opened. It was like finding the magic button. Eddie tried it again. Every time he touched the lower lip, the mouth opened, like the doors of an elevator.

Touch, open, slurp, gulp. Touch, open, slurp, gulp.

This wasn't so bad, Eddie decided, and he actually began to enjoy it. He sang as he shoved in the beets. He made funny little noises in his throat. He growled like a bear, clucked like a chicken, whistled and barked. This was the life. The job was easy, simple, and there was nobody around to tell him what to do. He threw back his head and crowed like a rooster.

Herman stopped swallowing. His eyes narrowed and slowly his lips began stretching in a wide smile. Thin trickles of red goo oozed from the corners of his mouth and onto his bib.

"Oh, no!" said Eddie. "Don't smile, Herman. Please don't smile! It wasn't really funny! I didn't mean it."

And then the baby sneezed.

It was like an explosion. Red guk dripped from Eddie's hair, his nose, his cheeks, and Herman himself looked like an accident victim. It was as though half his lunch had been shot from guns.

EDDIE'S EYE FELL on the jar of creamed spinach on the counter. That must be the second course. The poor kid must be a vegetarian. In went a spoonful of spinach on top of the strained beets, and when Herman sneezed again, he looked like a Christmas tree. So did Eddie.

By the time the spinach was gone, Herman's appetite had actually increased. He bounced with anticipation, banged his spoon on the tray, and or-

dered his next course in what was obviously Portuguese, accented with a burp.

Eddie scraped the last bit of beets and spinach from the jars, poured a cup of milk for Herman, and waited. Maybe the hunger would go away. Maybe he was on a diet, and Mrs. O'Conner didn't want him to have anymore.

"You've had enough, Herman," Eddie said. "That's it, old fella."

Herman bounced up and down even harder. His red and green mouth opened wide, and he gave a bellow that rattled the clock on the wall. The bellow was followed by a shriek and then a roar, and because he kept twisting around toward the zwieback box on the table, Eddie decided that Herman was used to having milk and toast for dessert, so he gave him a slice.

Herman didn't eat it, really. He mangled it, mauled it, smashed it, pounded it, and ground it into the seams and crevices of his high chair. He held it with his thumb tucked under, turned it at right angles to his mouth, and rammed it up his nostrils.

Eddie covered his eyes. Herman the Terrible was enjoying his dessert very much, but Eddie couldn't bear to watch. When he finally looked, there was nothing left but a soggy crust. Herman dropped it in his milk, stuck his fist in on top of it, and lifted the whole thing over his head upside down.

The O'Conners' kitchen, Eddie decided, should be declared a disaster area. The first thing to do was to clean up Herman and take care of the floor later. He began to wish that Dink and Elizabeth were here to divide up the work.

He lifted Herman from the high chair. There was a puddle of milk on the seat. Eddie set the baby on the counter beside the sink, holding him tightly with one hand, and reached for the washcloth with the other.

There were crumbs in Herman's hair, his ears, and the folds of his fat neck. There was even zwieback in his eye lashes, and his pudgy fingers were glued together with creamed spinach.

It took four washings to get the baby clean, and Eddie had to take off all Herman's wet sticky clothes and put on his pajamas. He changed his diaper while he was at it, and then closed the kitchen door so he wouldn't have to look at the place. It made him sick. He stuck Herman in the playpen while he cleaned himself up.

"Well, Herman," he said finally. "What do you want to do now? Look. Here's a book about the three little pigs." He picked up the baby, set him on his lap and put the book in front of them.

Pow! Down came Herman's fist on the little pig

who built his house out of straw.

Bam! Down came the other fist on the little pig who built his house out of sticks.

Wham! Down came Herman's head on the little pig who built his house out of bricks.

"Didn't like that story, huh?" said Eddie. "Okay."

He placed the baby on the rug and put on a record called *Big Rock Candy Mountain.* As soon as Burl Ives began to sing, Herman the Terrible began to bray. The louder the singing, the stronger the bellow. If any of the windows were open, Eddie thought, the neighbors would probably call the police. He looked at the clock. Two more hours before the O'Conners came home.

At NINE-THIRTY, Eddie decided that Herman should be getting sleepy. At least he hoped that Herman was sleepy.

"Sleepy, Herman?" he asked.

The big baby glared at him and growled.

Eddie picked him up and started for the bedroom. The baby screamed. He kicked and waved his arms and banged his head against Eddie's chest. *Whap!* He gave Eddie a wallop on the chin. It was all Eddie could do to keep from dropping him, but he held on tightly and put him in his crib.

Herman kicked at the slats of his crib. He punched his fists against the headboard. He banged his head against the mattress. Eddie sat down beside the crib and tried to sing to Herman. Herman threw a rubber duck and hit him on the ear.

"Well, goodnight," said Eddie at last, turning out the lamp, and he went into the hall and closed the door.

Herman let out a shriek. It sounded like an air raid siren. It rose and fell, growing louder and louder all the time. Maybe he needed another diaper change. Eddie went back in the room and changed his diaper. Herman watched him all the while with big brown eyes, but as soon as Eddie left, the screaming began again. Maybe he needed a drink of water.

Eddie got a plastic cup, filled it with water, and took it to the baby. *Swat!* Herman sent it flying. There was water all over the dresser, the rug, the walls, and the toy chest.

This time Eddie didn't say anything. He got a towel and wiped up the water. Then he went back outside and closed the door. Herman continued to scream.

It was scary somehow, being alone with a baby and listening to him scream like that. Eddie didn't know what was the matter. He didn't know if it was normal or not. He wished someone was around to tell him what to do. The responsibility was enormous.

After five minutes, the yelling stopped suddenly. The house was strangely quiet. Maybe Herman had put something in his mouth and was choking to death. Maybe he had stuck his head through the slats of the crib and was strangling. Maybe he had fallen out of bed and had a brain concussion.

Slowly Eddie crept to the door and put his ear to the crack. He listened for sounds of breathing. Nothing. Maybe he ought to check. Maybe another minute and it would be too late.

He opened the door.

Whap! A teddy bear hit him on the other ear, and there were Herman's eyes, glaring at him from the darkness of the crib.

Eddie closed the door again and went back in the living room to read his own book. He had read only one paragraph, however, when he heard a very strange sound from the bedroom. It was as though someone were moving the furniture. Eddie listened. *Creakity, slide. Creakity slide.* Eddie tried to ignore it, but it went on and on.

He got up and went back to the door. He turned the knob but the door wouldn't open. Something was in front of it. His heart raced. Herman the

Terrible, Herman the Strong, Herman the Awful must have climbed out of bed and pushed the dresser in front of the door.

In panic, Eddie shoved with all his might. The door moved and the crib with it. Herman the Terrible, standing at the front of his crib like a captain at the helm of his ship, had managed to rock and scoot the crib across the room.

Eddie pushed the crib back and Herman laughed delightedly in the darkness. Eddie took a diaper and tied one leg of the crib to the radiator.

"Herman," he said, looking the baby in the eye, "this is it. You can cry, you can bellow, you can stay awake all night if you want to, but the jig is up. And the sooner you go to sleep, the sooner you can wake up tomorrow and be terrible all over again."

Herman screamed, brayed, and rocked for a while longer, and then his voice began to give out. The bellow sounded a little frayed at the edges, a little softer, a little mushy. The rocking began to die down. Finally the big bad baby was crying a sleepy sing-song tune, and then there was no tune at all.

Once more Eddie crept to the bedroom. Once more he opened the door. There lay Herman, sound asleep with a thumb in his mouth. His knees were tucked under him, his rump was in the air, and somehow he looked very sweet and tender and small.

Even Herman couldn't be terrible all of the time, Eddie decided. Maybe in his dreams he was the nicest kid on the block.

Eddie went back to the living room to finish his book and then he remembered the kitchen. He opened the door and stood looking at it wearily . . . at the green stuff on the floor and the red stuff on the walls and the soggy gray stuff all over the high chair. The sitter was expected to leave the house in the same condition that he found it. Isn't that what the contract said?

Why had he ever wanted to be boss? Where was the simple, easy job he'd been looking for all his life? There wasn't any such thing, that's what. Work wasn't always excitement and fun and money. Sometimes it was just plain work. Sometimes you didn't want to do it at all, but you did, because it was your job.

And so, humming to himself, Eddie rolled up his sleeves, picked up the mop, and began.